**DO NOT REMOVE
CARDS FROM POCKET**

Grandma's Shoes

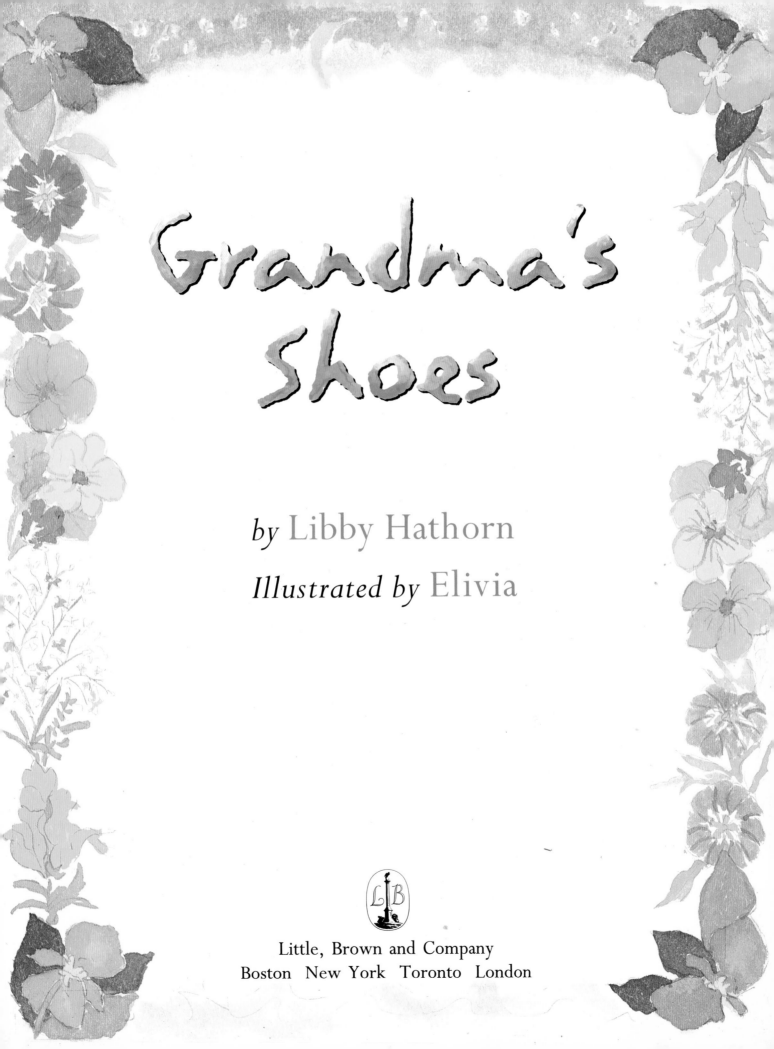

Grandma's Shoes

by Libby Hathorn

Illustrated by Elivia

Little, Brown and Company
Boston   New York   Toronto   London

In the memory of my grandmothers,
Margaret Emily and Edith Elizabeth,
and for grandmothers everywhere

L. H.

For my two beloved Sadyes,
my mother and my daughter,
who never got to meet
each other, here.
And with love for Grandpa Hayam,
who lived with us in the months I created
the illustrations for this book and who died
soon thereafter in South Africa.
Thank you for living long enough to
become important to Sadye.

E.

Text copyright © 1994 by Libby Hathorn
Illustrations copyright © 1994 by Elivia Savadier

First Edition

Library of Congress Cataloging-in-Publication Data
Hathorn, Elizabeth.
    Grandma's shoes / by Libby Hathorn ; illustrated by Elivia. — 1st
ed.
        p.   cm.
    Summary: A young girl copes with her grandmother's death with the
help of the old woman's shoes and some special memories.
    ISBN 0-316-35135-0
    [1. Grandmothers — Fiction. 2. Death — Fiction.] I. Savadier,
Elivia, ill. II. Title.
PZ7.H2843Gr   1994
[E] — dc20   93-20776

10 9 8 7 6 5 4 3 2 1

NIL

Printed in Italy

The paintings in this book were done in watercolor and pencil on Strathmore paper.
Text set in Perpetua by Typographic House and display type set in Lettrés Eclatées.

When Grandma died, lots of people came to our house.

"Who could ever step into such a woman's shoes?" the family asked.

"Who?" the friends and neighbors echoed, nodding sadly.

I wondered, too. Who could ever make our house so happy? Who could make the bright flowers bloom, the way she did? Who could braid my hair so well and hum so many tunes, one for every single hour of every single day, the way she could?

After the sighing and the talking and the crying, the family and the friends all came to my mother's table. But there was no laughter and feasting like on holidays. And there were none of Grandma's jokes. "Ah, who could ever fill such a woman's shoes?" they asked one another again and again.

Late at night, I lie all alone in the room I've always shared with my grandma. My mother and my aunts have taken Grandma's things away, leaving only her picture in a gold-colored frame on the dresser. It's a picture of a young Grandma and not the comfortable lined face I know. I turn it to the wall.

My mother comes to kiss me good night and to tell me that soon my little sister's bed will be moved in here beside mine. I nod, but I don't want to share my room with a baby. I want to share with my grandma, like always.

I lie still, listening for Grandma's breathing. I smell the fragrance of her rose scent, but I see her bedroom chair is empty of tomorrow's clothes.

"Grandma, where are you?" I say out loud to the quiet of the room, sitting up in my bed. Then, tucked back under the chair, I see Grandma's shoes. I jump out of bed and snatch up those shoes. I hug them, and the tears I thought were over and done with this sad day begin to fall again. I take the shoes back to bed with me so that I can sleep with them close by me.

In the morning, I set the shoes on the floor the way Grandma always does. I see they are too large for me, but I want to put them on. I sit on the side of the bed and I slide my feet into the shoes — giving a little sigh the way Grandma always does.

I balance in Grandma's shoes, and there's a sudden funny, swirly feeling. I'm no longer in my room with the big wardrobe and the window looking out onto Grandma's pots of begonias all in bloom. There's a rustling and sighing as if the wind is blowing, and I think — yes, any minute I'll hear her voice. Any minute I'll see her!

I am in the midst of a glowing forest. Leaves that have left home, as I have, swirl around me. Faces of flowers blaze at me. Big butterfly wings brush my cheek as her old hands so often did.

There is the smell of her garden so close — a sweet rottenness mingled with tender newness.

Ah, Grandma where are you?

But I cannot catch even a glimpse of her no matter where I search.

I come to a clearing where a thin strand of waterfall cries silvery tears. I am hot and tired. I stand right under that waterfall, and I cry, too.

Back in my room that afternoon, I remember Grandma's stories of the forest. The funny ones with the monkeys and the snakes, the scary ones with spiders and giant birds.

I think I will tell my mother and father all about the magic shoes. But when I bring the shoes out of my room, my father snatches them out of my hands and hides them behind a potted plant.

"You'll only make your mother sad," he says.

"But aren't we sad already?" I ask him.

A little later I creep out and get the shoes from behind the pot.

I take them into my room and place them carefully among the treasures that Grandma keeps at the bottom of the wardrobe and that only she and I know about — worn leather shoes among handworked Chinese bags, old English poetry books, a teeny-tiny Persian mat, a Russian babushka dolly, a small African drum, and fragrant boxes of Indian teas.

I love looking at Grandma's treasures, for each has its own story. But who will ever tell the stories now? I worry.

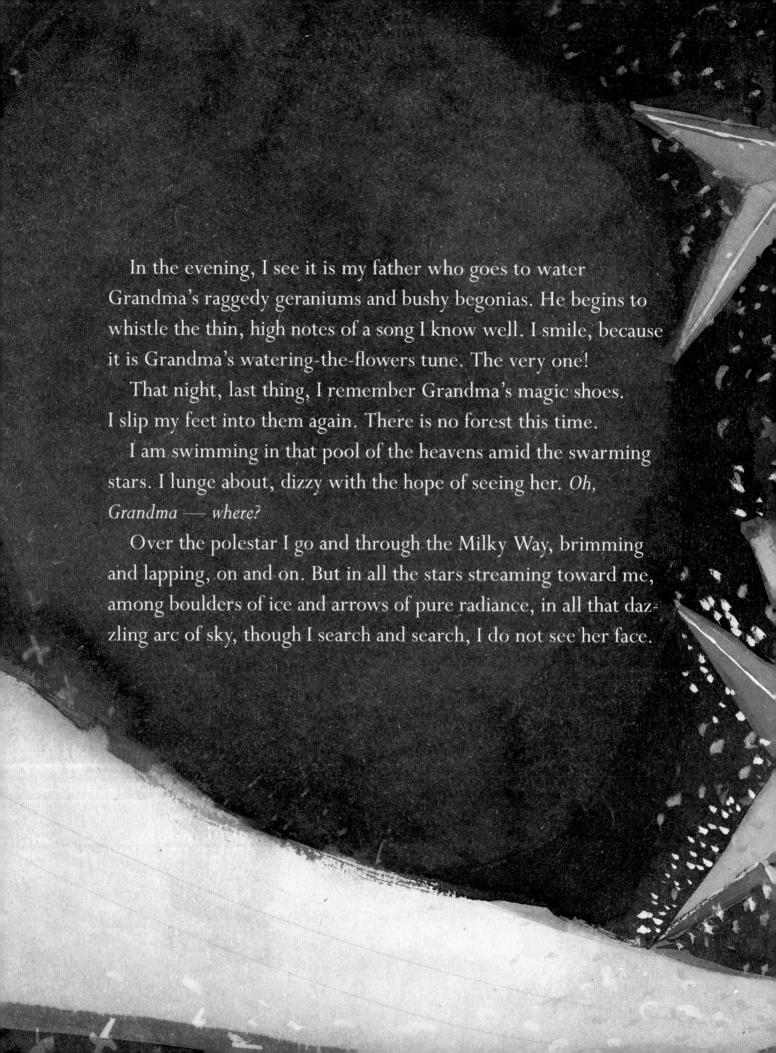

In the evening, I see it is my father who goes to water Grandma's raggedy geraniums and bushy begonias. He begins to whistle the thin, high notes of a song I know well. I smile, because it is Grandma's watering-the-flowers tune. The very one!

That night, last thing, I remember Grandma's magic shoes. I slip my feet into them again. There is no forest this time.

I am swimming in that pool of the heavens amid the swarming stars. I lunge about, dizzy with the hope of seeing her. *Oh, Grandma — where?*

Over the polestar I go and through the Milky Way, brimming and lapping, on and on. But in all the stars streaming toward me, among boulders of ice and arrows of pure radiance, in all that dazzling arc of sky, though I search and search, I do not see her face.

When I lift my feet out of her shoes, I gaze out the window. I remember more of Grandma's stories and the way she would point things out to me in that small piece of the sky above us that she always called ours.

My mother bakes the scented herb bread next day, and I think it is Grandma clattering about and singing in the kitchen. I go as I always do, and my mother breaks off the hot crusts for me.

"Your father tells me you have Grandma's shoes in your room," my mother says. "One day soon when your feet have grown they'll fit you. And then if you like, you can try them."

I do not tell my mother that I am already trying Grandma's shoes from time to time.

I wait until last thing that night to slide my feet slowly, slowly into the shoes once more. No forest. No starry heavens either.

But I hear singing as I go whirling over seas and cities and rivers and mountains. Yes, it is Grandma singing! And the song calls me down and down to a dark blue lake.

Oh I am falling, falling into the lake and now through the lake! And ahead there is such a fiery brightness, like the very heart of a volcano! *Oh, Grandma, help!* But I pass by into a new velvety darkness that is all wrapped around with her voice.

"Grandma, Grandma!" I yell with joy, for at last I can see her coming toward me. "I've found you! Come home, Grandma, now!"

"You have found me little one, it is true. But the time of telling stories, growing flowers, and braiding your hair — that is past."

"Oh, please come back to us, Grandma," I say, hearing the seriousness of her words.

"I can't come back," she tells me gently. And then she smiles
again in that old familiar way. "Besides, I like it here."

"Then I will stay right here with you," I tell her, but she shakes her head.

"No, not here. The trees and the stars, the mountains, and the silver waterfall — they do not need you yet. You must go back. And you must do what I tell you in all things."

For a moment I feel angry. But I know that I will do whatever she asks of me.

"I want you to put those shoes of mine right at the back of the big old wardrobe. When your feet have grown big enough to wear them, you will be a child no longer. I promise you that then they'll be your shoes. Truly your shoes. You will do this, won't you?"

I nod yes, although I feel hot tears. And I reach out to hug her good-bye, but already she is gone.

Next morning, my mother asks me to braid my sister's hair. She wriggles about and is impatient, just like I was when I was little. So I tell her the story of Grandma's magic shoes.

I tell her of all the wonderful places I have searched to find our grandma and how happy I am now because I know just where she is. My sister is too little to understand very much, but she must like the words.

She sits very, very still as I tell.

Soon, when she comes into my room to share with me, I'll show her Grandma's treasures, one by one. And I'll tell her Grandma's stories, one by one. And some new ones of my own. She'll like that.

But I won't show her the magic shoes yet. Not until the day my feet fit them perfectly. For on that day, oh, on that day, just as it was promised, I know it — *I will be the one who steps into Grandma's shoes!*